THE SPRING SUIT

P. G. WODEHOUSE

THE SPRING SUIT

THE SPRING SUIT

Rosie was going to buy a new spring suit for George's birthday. Looking at that sentence again, I see that it could be open to misconstruction. The suit was for herself. But it was to be bought in honour of George's birthday and flashed before his admiring gaze for the duration of that occasion. Altogether, taking it all round, George Mellon's twenty–first birthday promised to be one of the biggest things in history. In the afternoon he was going to strike his employer for a raise, in the evening he and Rosie would dine at the McAstor instead of the red–ink place they usually frequented, and at night they would take in a show, with possibly a bite of supper afterwards at a cabaret place.

A formidable program, and one that made it imperative that Rosie's dress should not be out of the picture. She had been saving all the winter to buy a really irreproachable suit, and the money was in the bank, straining at the leash. All that remained was to make a good selection.

You probably know Rosie by sight. She sits in a sort of kiosk in front of one of those motion picture palaces that have sprung up in recent years like a rash on the face of our fair city. You hand your money in through a little pigeonhole in the glass front of her den and she presses a button, causing a cardboard ticket to leap at you out of a brass slab. Thus far you may argue that I have not sufficiently identified Rosie, New York being full of girls who do conjuring tricks in glass cages.

True, since the movie delirium set in, there are a great many girls who do this. But Rosie is the one who smiles. The others give you your ticket with a sort of aloof hauteur. They have a resigned air, as if the spectacle of multitudes wasting money on the movies saddened them. If they spoke you feel that they would say: "Oh, well, what's the use? There's one born every minute!"

Rosie is different. Rosie beams at you. She has a cheerful little face, with a nice wide mouth; and when you push your hard–earned money through the opening in the glass a flash of white teeth encourages you to believe that, after all, you may not be going to waste your evening, and that you will not subsequently kick your spine up through your hat for having been such a chump as to pay thirty good cents to see Mabelle Gooch—or whoever it is—tumble over herself in Lepers of the Great White Way, or whatever the picture is called. You go in feeling heartened, with a vague impression that Rosie must be a rather nice girl.

THE SPRING SUIT

George Mellon, the party of the second part, is also, curiously enough, a door hound, a keeper of the gates and a dweller upon the threshold. But he works by day. He is the presentable young man who sits in the anteroom at the offices of the Ladies' Sphere and keeps people from seeing the editor. Editors, who are human beavers, industrious little creatures who work hard and shrink from the public gaze, generally employ, to insure privacy, a small boy with red hair, a tight suit and an air of having seen all the trickery and wickedness in the world.

At the Ladies' Sphere, however, where beautiful and refined women are popping in and out all day like rabbits, something with a little more tone is required: and George landed the job against a field of twenty- six competitors. This should enable you to get an adequate angle on George. It is not every young man who can head off without offense lovely creatures in Paris frocks and mink coats, and convince them simultaneously that it is the editor's dearest wish to have a long cozy chat with them, but that he can't see them this morning. Men with less diplomacy than George have held down ambassadorships in foreign capitals.

It was this manner of his that had first attracted Rosie when she had called one morning to see the editor.

"Have you an appointment, madam?" George had inquired, bending suavely over the little wooden gate with the air of a plenipotentiary at the Court of St. James exchanging compliments with a princess of the blood.

Rosie said she had no appointment.

"Then I fear," said George with manly regret, "that it will scarcely be possible for you to see Mr. Hebblethwaite to-day. Mr. Hebblethwaite is exceedingly busy just now. The magazine goes to press to-day." The magazine was always going to press when people tried to get past George. "If you would care to leave a message——"

"I only wanted to ask him if he would mind giving me the Ten Delicious Morsels From the Chafing Dish that he had in the March number. I cut them out, but I lost them."

"Our Circulation Department would attend to that," said George. "If you would care to leave your name and address I will see that they are forwarded to you."

THE SPRING SUIT

And in the short space of time it took Rosie to write down her name and address George had handed the raspberry to two artists and a short−story writer. Rosie felt that this was no ordinary man.

George must have conceived an equally flattering opinion of her; for that same evening he called at her rooming house in person, bearing the March number. And so pleasantly and swiftly did their acquaintance progress that, before he left, Rosie had cooked Delicious Morsel Number Three on her chafing dish, and they ate it together. Rosie was a wonderful cook; and it may be that George, who had suffered much from boarding−house meals since he came to New York, acquired at that moment his first yearning for domesticity.

All through the summer and fall their intimacy had ripened, and in the middle of November George proposed. They decided that they would get married immediately after his next raise of salary, and George had fixed the beginning of May as the date for negotiating that business deal. Balmy spring, with all its softening influences, would have had a chance by then to work on Mr. Hebblethwaite and render him malleable.

"But oh, George," said Rosie, "suppose he doesn't give it to you!"

"He will. He knows I'm a valuable man."

"Of course you are. But——"

"There were twenty−six others applied for the job same time as me, and I copped. That shows you."

"I know you're wonderful!" said Rosie. "But, still——"

Rosie had once traveled up in the elevator with Mr. Hebblethwaite and the memory lingered. The editor was a little man, with fiery eyes that glowed behind big spectacles, and he had glared at Rosie in the elevator as if the only thing that kept him from eating her was the fact that he had already breakfasted.

"It isn't everyone," said George, "who could do my job. You wouldn't believe the number of females who come every day to waste Mr. Hebblethwaite's time. I tell you, I wonder I don't lose my voice with telling them he's busy. And it's got to be done right, or you might as well not do it at all. You can't go offending people. But gee, you've no idea what an amount of gall women have! Why, the first week I was at the office a female got past me by saying she was the boss' wife. She looked all right, she spoke all right; so I thought she was all right, and I opened the gate. In about ten minutes out she came, said good morning with a nice smile, and beat it. And two seconds later I'm rung for and there's the boss chewing holes in the carpet and smashing up the furniture with his bare hands. Seems she was a lady book agent; and before he could get rid of her she had landed him with Historic Heartbreakers, highly educational and as interesting as a novel. Since then I've played it safe. No body gets past me without an appointment. The boss knows that, and values me according."

"But Mr. Hebblethwaite looks so fierce. I'd die of fright if I had to ask him for a raise."

George felt in his inner pocket and produced, with a certain complacence, a cutting from the advertising pages of the magazine that employed him.

"I might have felt that way once, but the other day I came across this. I've written for — the book. It looks to me like the goods."

The cutting showed a picture of a resolute young man with a clean–cut face and a strong mouth pointing a minatory finger at an elderly man with a pointed beard. The elderly man was cowering down in his chair and obviously getting the loser's end of the mix up. Beneath the picture were the words: "Look Him in the Eye and Win!"

And then:

No matter how big he is, no matter how powerful, he will listen, heed you and respect you. Don't flinch. Make him drop his glance or turn his gaze and your battle is won. What battle? Your every battle—the battle you must fight every day with the men who block your way to success.

Have courage and show it. "Courage for what?" you ask. The courage to assert yourself, to demand and get your rights; the calm, steady, unwavering courage that shows through your eye to every man you meet.

THE SPRING SUIT

Send the coupon below and let us mail to you—absolutely free, for examination—a copy of this sensational new book—The Will and its Training: by Otis Elmer Banks, Ph.D.

Have courage and the world is your oyster.

Rosie was impressed.

"Why should the world be an oyster?" she asked.

"I don't know," said George frankly. "I didn't understand that bit myself. But that's not the point. The whole thing is that I mean to train myself scientifically and then go to it. You can see by what it says here that it'll be like taking money from a child's bank. Very likely I shan't hardly have to ask. Probably he'll unbelt directly he meets my eye."

So that was settled; and it seemed to Rosie to make it all the more imperative that she should not fall down on her end of the coming campaign. If George was going to go through an ordeal like that for her sake, the least she could do was to reward him by being a credit to him in the matter of a spring suit. She was in the position of the lady for whom a knight jousted in the Middle Ages. After a hard afternoon at the tournament the knight had a right to expect to find his queen of beauty looking worth the trouble. As the days went by, Rosie began to regard the spring suit as a sort of symbol of her love and of her worthiness to be loved. Her future seemed to hang on it.

The process of buying a spring suit, especially if you wait till spring to do it, is not so simple as it might seem to the lay mind. The big room at the big store that Rosie had selected was crammed to suffocation when she arrived. Women of all sorts and sizes were competing for the attention of the salesgirls. The assemblage looked like the mob scene in a motion picture. Large women jostled small women; short women jostled tall women; thin women and stout women pushed one another and everybody else impartially.

Rosie sat down in a corner to wait. It was the first warm day of spring and she felt exhausted. But because she was Rosie and combined an out—size in hearts with a small size in bodies, it was not her own tiredness that compelled her pity. She was sorry for the salesgirls. They were working so terribly hard. Rosie watched them dive into mysterious closets, come out laden with suits and more suits, and exhibit these to the customers in much the same manner as the waiter at your restaurant shows you the lobster, but without the latter's optimism.

The waiter is confident and cheery. He knows there is going to be a happy ending. His air is the air of a man concluding the last trading formalities of a successful business operation. But these girls who were parading spring suits had the disheartening knowledge, the fruit of long experience, that they were probably wasting their time, and that most of the women they served had no intention of buying but had merely come there to play at shopping.

Presently the crowd thinned. It was near closing time. The big room presented an after–the–battle appearance. Spring suits lay about on tables as if they had swooned there from exhaustion. The air was close and heavy. The salesgirls stood in twos and threes among the wreckage like the survivors of a forlorn hope. One of them perceived Rosie and limped toward her in a depressed way. Rosie could almost see her thinking. Plainer than words her pale face was saying: "Oh, Lord! Another of them!"

"Can I attend to you, madam?"

Rosie felt shrinkingly apologetic. She had forgotten that she had a headache herself and that she had been waiting patiently for nearly an hour. She only felt that it was brutal of her to keep the poor girl working a moment longer. "I want to look at suits, please."

The salesgirl's expression seemed to say that her worst fears had been confirmed.

"What size, madam?" she said mechanically.

"Eighteen misses' please," said Rosie meekly, feeling like an overbearing Eastern tyrant.

The girl walked slowly away, picked up one of the suits that had fainted on a near–by chair, and returned, her listlessness more marked than ever. She resembled someone who had been forced into playing a game that through much repetition has become tedious and painful.

The suit she bore was, in a sense, a suit. In shape and material it conformed to the definition. But the mere sight of it sent a shudder through Rosie, by so much did it miss being the ideal of her dreams. It had no poetry, no meaning, no *chic*, no *je−ne−sais−quoi*, no anything that was attractive and inspiring. Worse, it looked vulgar. It was a loud black−and−white check, and one glance told Rosie that she would look awful in it. She had opened her lips to denounce and reject the horrid thing when she caught sight of the girl's face.

Girls who live alone and support themselves, like Rosie, come to acquire something of the masculine attitude towards life. They lose the woman's inborn gift of shopping and acquire in its place that consideration for the other party to the transaction which marks the average male. A man whose aim it is to buy a pair of trousers does not stand coolly by while the attendant exhibits his entire stock and then go off without making a purchase. A brief "Gimme those!" and his shopping is finished.

Rosie had this male characteristic. She hated giving trouble. Even in ordinary circumstances it pained her to have to refuse to buy. And now, looking at this pale tired girl before her, she forgot all about the vital importance of finding the one spring suit heaven had destined for her from the beginning of things. All she felt was that she must get the business finished quickly and let the poor girl go home.

"That will do splendidly," she said.

The salesgirl blinked. This was one of the things that didn't happen. Then, as realization came to her, her eyes lit up. Their grateful gleam was Rosie's recompense. And she needed some recompense, for directly the words were out of her mouth she knew what she had done.

The memory of a kind action is supposed to be an unfailing receipe for happiness. Boy Scouts grow fat on it. But Rosie, as she went to meet George at the Hotel McAstor on the night of his birthday, felt none of that glow of quiet content she might reasonably have expected as her right. On the contrary, she was miserable and apprehensive. Man—which includes woman—being the ruler of creation and having an immortal soul and other advantages, ought to be superior to such trivalities as clothes.

A quiet conscience is more important than a loud suit. But such is human frailty that the best of us lose our nerve if we feel that our outer husk is not all it should be. Rosie knew that she did not look right! And when a woman feels that, she might just as well go home and get into a kimono.

The situation was rendered more poignant by the fact that George was not as other men. George was employed at the offices of a magazine that dictated the fashions to a million women; where even the stenographers looked like fashion plates and every caller presented to his gaze the last word in what was smart.

George, therefore, naturally had a high standard. Something special was required to win his trained approval. And she was coming to meet him at a fashionable restaurant in a black–and–white check suit that was not only hideous but hardly respectable.

It was just the sort of suit that girls wore to whom strange men on street corners said: "Hello, kiddo!" It was a flashy, giggling, sideways–glancing, chorus–of–a–burlesque–show sort of suit. It was the outer covering of a cutie and a baby doll.

As she got off the car she saw him waiting outside the restaurant. He looked superb. George was always a great dresser. He was tall and slim, and resembled those divine youths you see in tailors' advertisements, who stand with bulging bosoms and ingrowing waists, saying to their college chums, as they light a cigarette: "Yes, my dear chap, I always buy the Kute–kut Klothes, each suit guaranteed for one year on the easy–payment system. A fellow must look decent!"

She hurried toward him with a sinking heart, gamely forcing her face into a smile.

"Here I am, dear!"

"Hello!" said George.

Was his voice cold? Was his manner distant?

"Many happy returns of the day!"

"Thanks!"

THE SPRING SUIT

Yes. His voice was cold. His manner was distant. And a dull disapproving look was in his eyes.

There was a momentary silence. They stood aside to allow a stream of diners to go in. Rosie looked at the women. They were walking reproaches to her. They were smart. They glittered. A sudden panic came upon her. Something told her that George would be ashamed to be seen with her in a place like the McAstor.

"I say, Rosie!"

There was embarrassment in George's voice. He gave a swift look over his shoulder into the crowded prismatic lobby of the restaurant.

"I don't know that I'm so crazy to have dinner here," he said awkwardly. "How about going somewhere else?"

The blow had fallen. And, like most blows that fall after we have been anticipating them, it had an unexpected effect on its victim. A moment before she had felt humble, ashamed of herself. But now, when George had come out into the open and as good as told her in so many words that he shrank from being seen with her in public, a fighting spirit she had never suspected herself of possessing flamed into being. All her unhappiness crystallized into a furious resentment. She hated George, who had humiliated her.

"I don't mind," she said.

"Darned noisy crowded place," said George. "I've heard the service is bad too."

She despised him now, besides hating him. It was pitiful to see him standing there, mumbling transparent lies to try to justify himself.

"Shall we go to Giuseppe's?" she asked coldly.

The question was a test. Giuseppe's was where they always went, one of the four hundred and eighty-seven Italian restaurants in the neighborhood of Times Square which provided sixty-cent table-d'hote dinners for the impecunious. The food was plentiful, especially the soup, which was a meal in itself, and they had always enjoyed themselves there; but if George could countenance the humble surroundings of Giuseppe's on his birthday, on the night they had been looking forward to for weeks as a grand occasion, then George must indeed have sunk low. For George to answer "Yes" was equivalent to an admission that he had feet of clay.

"Yes," answered George; "that's just what I'd like."

Rosie put her finger in her mouth and bit it hard. It was the only way she could keep from crying.

Dinner was a miserable affair. The constraint between them was like a wall of fog. It was perhaps fortunate that they had decided to go to Giuseppe's, for there conversation is not essential. What with the clatter of cutlery, the babel of talk, the shrill cries of the Italian waitresses conveying instruction and reproof to an unseen cook, who replied with what sounded like a recitative passage from grand opera, and the deep gurgling of the soup dispatchers, there is plenty of tumult to cover any lack of small talk.

Rosie, listening to the uproar, with the chair of the diner behind her joggling her back and the elbow of the diner beside her threatening her ribs, remembered with bitterness that George had called the McAstor a noisy crowded place.

When the ice cream and the demi−tasses appeared Rosie leaned forward.

"Did you get tickets for a theater?" she asked.

"No," said George; "I thought I'd wait and see what show you'd like to go to."

"I don't think I want to go to a show. I've got a headache. I'll go home and rest."

"Good idea!" said George. It was hopeless for him to try to keep the relief out of his voice. "I'm sorry you've got a headache."

Rosie said nothing.

They parted at her door in strained silence. Rosie went wearily up to her room and sat down on the accommodating piece of furniture that was a bed by night and by day retired modestly into the wall and tried to look like a bookshelf. She had deceived George when she told him she had a headache. Her head had never been clearer. Never had she been able to think so coherently and with such judicial intensity. She could see quite plainly now how mistaken she had been in George. She had been deceived by the glamour of the man. She did not blame herself for this. Any girl might have done the same.

Even now, though her eyes were opened, she freely recognized his attractions. He was good–looking, an entertaining talker, and superficially kind and thoughtful. She was not to be blamed for having fancied herself in love with him; she ought to consider herself very lucky to have found him out before it was too late. She had been granted the chance of catching him off his guard, of scratching the veneer, and she felt thankful. . . . At this point in her meditations Rosie burst into tears—due, no doubt, to relief.

The drawback to being a girl who seldom cries is that when you do cry you do it clumsily and without restraint. Rosie was subconsciously aware that she was weeping a little noisily; but it was not till a voice spoke at her side that she discovered she was rousing the house.

"For the love of Pete, honey, whatever is the matter?"

A stout, comfortably unkempt girl in a pink kimono was standing beside her. There was concern in her pleasant face.

"It's nothing," said Rosie. "I didn't mean to disturb you."

"Nothing! It sounded like a coupla families being murdered in cold blood. I'm in the room next to this; and I guess the walls in this joint are made of paper, for it sounded to me as if it was all happening on my own rug. Come along, honey! You can tell me all about it. Maybe it's not true, anyway."

She sat down beside Rosie on the bookcase bed and patted her shoulder in a comforting manner. Then she drew from the recesses of her kimono a packet of chewing gum, a girl's best friend.

"Have some?"

THE SPRING SUIT

Rosie shook her head.

"Kind o' soothing, gum is," said the stout girl, inserting a slab into her mouth as if she were posting a letter, and beginning to champ rhythmically, like an amiable cow. "Now what's your little trouble?"

"There's nothing to tell."

"Well, go ahead and tell it, then."

Rosie gave in to the impulse that urged her to confide. There was something undeniably appealing and maternal about this girl. In a few broken sentences she revealed the position of affairs. When she came to the part where George had refused to take her into the McAstor the stout girl was so moved that she swallowed her gum and had to take another slab.

The stout girl gave it as her opinion that George was a cootie.

"Of course," said Rosie with a weak impulse to defend her late idol, "he's very particular about clothes."

The stout girl would hear no defense. She said it was Bolsheviki like George who caused half the trouble in the world. It began to look to her as if George Mellon was one of these here now lounge lizards that you read pieces about in the papers.

"Not," she said, eying Rosie critically, "but what that certainly is some little suit you've got on. I'll say so! Nobody couldn't look her best in that." She gave a sudden start. "Say, where did you get it?"

"At Fuller Benjamin's."

"No!" cried the stout girl. "But it is! I thought all along it looked kind o' familiar. Why, honey, that's the suit we girls call the Crown Prince, because it oughtn't to be at large! Why, it's a regular joke with us! I've tried to sell it a dozen times myself. What? Sure I work at Fuller Benjamin's. And—say, I remember you now. You came in just on closing time and Sadie Lewis waited on you. For the love o' Pete, why ever did you go and be so foolish as to let Sadie wish a quince like that on you?"

"She looked so tired," said Rosie miserably, "I just hated to bother her to show me a lot of suits; so I took the first. It seemed such a shame. She looked all worn out."

For the first time in her career as a chewer, a career that had covered two decades, the stout girl swallowed her gum twice in a single evening. Only the supremest emotion could have made her do this, for she was a girl who was careful of her chewing gum, even to the extent of parking it under the counter or behind doors for future use when it was not in active service.

When she bought gum she bought the serial rights. But now, in the face of this extraordinary revelation, swallowing it seemed the only thing to do. She was stunned. A miracle had happened. With her own eyes she had seen a shopper who had consideration for shopgirls. Diogenes could not have been more surprised if he had found his honest man.

"Well, if that don't beat everything!" she gasped. "Wherever did you get those funny ideas of yours about us salesladies being human? Didn't you know we was just machines? Now you listen here, honey: There's certainly something coming to you for that, and here's where you're going to get it. I've the cutest suit all tucked away down at the store, just ready and waiting for you. Honest, it's a bird! What's your size? Eighteen misses', I should judge. Why, it'll fit you just like mother made. I sold it this morning to a dame who went dippy over it."

"It's sold!"

"Don't you worry about that. It hasn't been sent off yet. And I know the dame that got her hooks onto it. She's one of the Boomerang Sisters, the kind you send goods to and have 'em come whizzing back to you. She's a C. O. D. lizard. She ain't worthy of that suit, honey, and she ain't going to get it. She'll get the Crown Prince instead and be told that's what she ordered."

"But won't you get into trouble?"

15

THE SPRING SUIT

"There you go again, worrying yourself about the poor working girl! Say, that habit's going to grow on you if you don't watch out! I won't get into no trouble. She'll let out a squawk you'll be able to hear as far as White Plains, I've no doubt; but I should manifest concern! I'm quitting on the seventeenth. Going to be married!"

The stout girl sighed dreamily.

"Say, there's a fellow that really is a fellow! Runs a dry–goods–and– notions store back home where I come from; been crazy about me since we were kids; has a car, coupla help, half–acre lot back of the house, twenty–eight chickens, and a bulldog that he's been offered fifty dollars for, and grows his own vegetables. I'm the lucky girl, all right. Not a thing to it!

"Well, you look in at the store bright and early to–morrow morning, ask for me—Miss Merridew's my name—and I'll have that suit waiting for you. I'll say good night now. Got to write to my boy before I hit the hay. See you later!"

The stout girl withdrew. Presently Rosie heard her through the wall singing Poor Butterfly. A little later there came an imperious banging on the floor above, from the room where the long–haired young man lived who was supposed to be writing a play. The singing stopped. Silence reigned.

George was dealing with a poetess in his suave manner when Rosie reached the office of the Ladies' Sphere at noon next day. In a few moments the poetess had receded like a brightly colored wave that rolls down the beach. The elevator engulfed her and she was no more. George came over to Rosie.

"Hello, kiddie! Where did you spring from?"

This was quite a different George. His eyes shone with pleasure at the sight of her. His animation had returned—a very different George from the dull–eyed disapproving critic of last night.

Rosie looked at him steadily, without an answering smile. She was a very different Rosie, also, from the stricken creature who had parted from him yesterday. The new suit was all and more than Miss Merridew had claimed for it. Navy blue, with short shoulders, tight sleeves and wonderful lines, it was precisely the suit of which Rosie had dreamed.

She felt decently clad at last. From the smart little straw hat, with its flowers and fruit, to the black silk stockings, with their white clocks, and the jaunty patent–leather pumps, she was precisely all that a girl would wish to be. She could hold up her head again.

And she did hold up her head, with a militant tilt of the chin. She was feeling strong and resolute. Before she left, the engagement would be broken. On that point she was as rigid as steel. If her outward appearance was all that George valued, she had done with him.

"I came to say something to you, George," she said quietly.

George did not appear to have heard her. He looked about him. From behind doors came the click of typewriters and the sound of voices, but nobody was visible. They had the anteroom to themselves.

"Say! I got it!"

"Got it?"

"The raise! Another fifteen per."

"Yes?"

He seemed not to notice the coolness of her voice. This man was full of his own petty triumph.

"I'll tell you one thing, though," he went on; "I don't know who Elmer Otis Banks is, but he's a prune! That dope of his may be all right with some people, but when it comes to slipping one over on Mr. Hebblethwaite it's about as much good as a cold in the head.

"Yesterday afternoon I breezed into the boss' office, looked him in the eye as per schedule, and said I could do with a raise. According to the dope he ought to have come across like a lamb. But all he did was to tell me to get out. I got out. The way I figured it was that if I didn't get out then I'd be getting out a little later for keeps."

THE SPRING SUIT

A caller intruded, desirous of seeing the editor. George disposed of her. He returned to Rosie.

"Well, back I go to my chair out here, feeling good and sore, and presently a dame blows in and wants to see the boss. I tell her nothing doing.

" 'You evidently don't know who I am,' she says, looking at me as if I was just one of the common people. 'I am Mrs. Hebblethwaite.'

"She had a book under her arm and it looked to me like a sample. I wasn't taking any chances.

" 'Sorry, ma'am,' I says, 'but the last Mrs. Hebblethwaite that made a play round the end and scored a touchdown in the boss' private office was a book agent. So unless you have an appointment, it's no go. I value my job and I want to hold it.'

" 'I shall speak to my husband about your impertinence,' she said, and beat it.

"I thought no more about it. And that night, while I was waiting for you in the McAstor lobby, I'm darned if the boss didn't come in with this same woman; and I heard her ask him if he'd remembered to put the cover over the canary's cage before they left home.

"Gee! By the time you arrived I'd made up my mind it would be the gate for me first thing this morning. I don't suppose you noticed anything, but I was feeling so sick I just wanted to creep away and die."

Rosie leaned bonelessly against the rail. The reaction from her militant mood had left her limp. The thought of how she had wronged her golden−hearted George filled her with self−loathing. She had no right to be engaged to the most perfect of his sex.

"Oh, George!" she gasped.

George misinterpreted her emotion. He patted her hand encouragingly.

"It's all right, kiddie! I told you there was a happy ending. This morning the boss sent for me.

THE SPRING SUIT

" 'What's all this I hear about your refusing Mrs. Hebblethwaite admittance yesterday?' he said. I was feeling that all was over now except the tearful farewells. 'She told you who she was,' he said. 'What did you keep her out for?'

" 'I thought you were busy, Mr. Hebblethwaite,' I said. 'And it's always been my idea that if callers hadn't appointments you weren't to be disturbed on any account.'

"He didn't say anything for a bit; then he kind of glared at me.

" 'How many were there after the job when you got it?'

"I told him twenty–seven, counting me.

" 'Then let me tell you, young man,' he said, worrying his cigar, 'that I don't consider you one of twenty–seven. You're one in a million! You've a head! Weren't you boring me yesterday with some silly story about wanting a raise? What do you want a raise for?'

" 'Want to get married, sir.' He looked at me in a pitying sort of way.

" 'You don't know when you're well off,' he said. 'Oh, well! Give this to the cashier.'

"And he scribbled something on a bit of paper. And—"

George broke off and slid nimbly to intercept a fair creature in mauve who was trying to buck center.

"Have you an appointment, madam? Then I fear—— Mr. Hebblethwaite is extremely busy. . . . The magazine goes to press to–day. If you will leave a message——"

He came back.

"What was I saying? Oh, yes. He gave me a note to the cashier for another fifteen a week. So there we are! Say, I happened to be passing a shop a few days ago and I saw in the window some parlor furniture—"

Rosie gulped.

THE SPRING SUIT

"But, George, why didn't you tell me?"

"Tell you? I have told you!"

"Last night, I mean."

George laughed a little sheepishly.

"Well, after the way I'd been blowing to you about what a marvel I was and what I was going to do to the boss when I got him alone, I kind of felt you'd think me such a darned fool. Besides, I didn't want to worry you."

"But you did worry me. I nearly died."

George stared.

"Eh? How? Why?"

"Why. I naturally thought, when you suddenly didn't want to go into the McAstor, that you were ashamed to be seen with me."

"Ashamed to be seen with you! Whatever gave you that idea?"

"I thought you thought my dress was too awful."

"What's the matter with your dress?" asked George, puzzled. "It looks all right to me."

"Not this one, the one I wore last night."

"Isn't that the one you wore last night?" said George.

"I never notice what you've got on, kiddie. You could wear overalls and make a hit with me. It's you I'm in love with, not the scenery."

Rosie blinked.

THE SPRING SUIT

"You're the most wonderful man on earth!"

"Sure! But don't tell anybody."

"But all the same, you're pretty awful not to see that this is the cutest spring suit ever made."

George looked into her eyes. Elmer Otis Banks himself never directed into anybody's eyes such a steady whole–hearted gaze. Looking over his shoulder again to make sure that their privacy was still undisturbed, he kissed Rosie.

"Anything you wear looks that way to me," he said. "Well, as I was saying, I was passing this shop, and there in the window was the swellest set of parlor furniture——"

Printed in the United Kingdom
by Lightning Source UK Ltd.
114570UKS00002B/126